THE
ISLAND
OF
SKREE

MW00743640

THE Jungle OF UTT

A series of adventure stories

This book belongs to

THE JUNGLE OF UTT

THE SECOND BOOK

MYSTERY OF THE LAKE

Written by Cameron Thomas

Illustrations by Andrej Krystoforski

When it's holiday time on the Island of Skree
A lot of the Utt people go off to the sea,
While for others, it's also quite pleasant to take
A stay-at-home holiday, down by the lake.
It was there, in the heat of a mid-July day
That a bunch of Utt youngsters had gone down to play,
When one boy suggested that they should all take
A swim to the far side of Utt Jungle lake.

The bear's son struck out for the opposite shore,
With the others behind him, a dozen or more,
They swam on quite happily, gay and light hearted,
When all of a sudden, the lake water parted.

It was then they all saw, not too far up ahead,
A strange looking creature which filled them with dread,
With a long blackened neck, and triangular head,
And where eyes should have been, balls of fire instead.
For a moment, they just didn't know what to do,
Then they raced for the shore very fast, wouldn't you?

And, with hardly a pause, ran to Utt Jungle Square,
To tell what they'd seen to the Utt Jungle Mayor,
They were all so excited, and made such a noise
By all talking at once, that he said, "Girls and boys
Just relax for a moment, cool down for a while,
Now, one at a time," he went on with a smile.

The young bear spoke first, he explained where they'd been,
And went on to describe the big "monster" they'd seen,
"It had a long neck that was all dark and slimy,
And eyes, big as saucers, all bloodshot and shiny.
There's no doubt it's a monster," the bear said, "It's true,"
And the others agreed, for they'd all seen it too.

When the boys had gone home, he went down to the shore,
And he searched for an hour and a half, maybe more.
But no sign of what they described could be seen;
The Utt Jungle Lake was quite calm and serene.

He returned to his office in Utt Jungle Square,
And the children, along with their parents, were there.
So he told them he thought that this "creature" just might
Be attracted, like moths, to a very bright light.
"So, let's each take a flare and go down to the shore,
And perhaps we will see what the young people saw."

Soon they stood round the lake with their torches held high
And they watched, and they waited, until, by and by,
From the lake's very middle, a dark shape was seen.
It was just where the children had said it had been.
But the creature, whatever it was floating there,
Was out of the range of the light from the flares.
And then Barnaby knew that to answer this riddle
He must get in a boat and row out to the middle.

So, Barnaby called for a volunteer crew,
And the bear said he'd go, and the Llamas did too,
And, each holding a flare, they rowed into the night
While Barnaby kept the dark shadow in sight.

Then, without any warning, they felt a hard crash,
And the boat tipped them into the lake, with a splash.
And the thing that they'd hit in the dark of the night
Slipped under the water and vanished from sight.

But the boat was still floating, and in half a minute
They had swum alongside and had pulled themselves in it.
Then they rescued the oars and they rowed back to land,
Where they built a big fire, right there on the sand.
They all sat around it, to get warm and dry,
When the Mayor had another idea to try.

It was early next day when the Mayor arose,
And went down to the lake with some unusual clothes,
A swim suit of rubber, and mask for his face,
So he could see clearly the floor of this place,
And a tank that strapped on, which was full of fresh air
To let him swim 'round in the water down there.

First the Llamas arrived, and then constable Bear,
And they asked him about all of those things lying there.
"It's a diving suit," Barnaby said with a grin,
"If he won't come to us, then I'll go down to him.
With this suit, I can go under water you see,
And by tugging this rope you can signal to me."

"But that's dangerous, isn't it sir?" asked the bear,
"You still don't know what might be lurking down there."
"I've a feeling," the Mayor said, "what we saw last night,
Won't look half so bad when it's seen in the light."

At the spot where the crash had upset them last night
The Mayor put the suit on, and zipped it up tight;
Then adjusting the face mask he said, "Here I go."
And he jumped into the water, and vanished below.

He was soon swimming 'round on the lake's sandy bed,
While the crew waited up in the boat overhead.
And he swam, and he searched, 'til he suddenly saw
The "creature" asleep on the lake's sandy floor.
Then he tied a strong line 'round the long blackened neck,
And he signalled his crewmen to pull him on deck.

"Now back to the shore," said the Mayor, "we must hurry,
And show all the people the cause of their worry.
We can drag him ashore on the end of this line,
But first, help me out of this wet suit of mine."

When they got to the shore, people gathered around
All anxious to see what the Mayor had found.
And they listened intently, as Barnaby said,
"Pull the line in, then you'll see the cause of your dread."
Yet some still were frightened of what it might be,
And afraid of the sight of the "monster" they'd see.

"Why, it's just some old wood," cried the boys on the shore,
"That's all that it is, bits of wood, nothing more."
"It's a piece of debris, from the old schoolhouse fire,"
Said Barnaby, "part of the roof and the spire.
And the fireball eyes were the brass pieces on it,
That glistened whenever the sun shone upon it."

"So you see, you were worried for nothing," he said,
"Still, I guess it does look like a neck and a head.
But it just goes to prove what I've told you before,
Don't be frightened of things that you don't know for sure.
So continue your swim, while the rest of us play,
I don't think you'll find any monsters today,
For monsters in lakes are unusual indeed."
And the Llamas in purple pyjamas agreed.

- BOOKS -

Published by:
MGT Publishing Inc.
207 Erskine Ave.
Toronto, Ontario
M4P-1Z5
Canada

Copyright:
The United States Copyright Office, The Library of Congress.

Copyright Office
Ottawa, Ontario, Canada

First published in 2002

ISBN 0-921800-02-9

Digitally Composed
by David Pereira

Printed in Hong Kong

Check out our web site at:
www.jungleofutt.com